Ashtray Etiquette

by Miranda Millar

To my family, for reading the same words over and over, for patiently surviving all the depression and manic episodes that led to this, and somehow never losing faith in the beauty of my madness.

To my friends, for being the fire beneath these words, and for showing me that inspiration comes from living boldly, even if it's messy and chaotic.

And to all the men who broke my heart—thank you for the destruction. You gave me pain, and I turned it into something far more useful than any of you ever could.

Introduction

This book doesn't need to be read in order. There's no plot, no perfectly arranged arc, no gold star for making it from the first page to the last without skipping. I actually encourage you not to read it straight through. Flip. Wander. Leave it in your bathroom and pick it up when something in your chest feels off. It's not a story. It's a cigarette break. A confession booth. A scrapbook of moments that didn't know where else to go.

I didn't sit down one day and decide to write a book. I bled into my notes app over years of unraveling. I wrote lines in the margins of receipts, in the backs of Ubers, on bar napkins and plane tickets and the kind of nights that never really end. These pages were written in pieces. Across apartments, across cities, across heartbreaks and hangovers. Some of them were written while deeply in love. Some while grieving. Some in a numb fog so thick I couldn't tell if I was writing or just trying to keep myself tethered to the world.

A lot of gin and wine went into this. An unknowable number of long French cigarettes—Capris, always Capris. I've smoked more of them than I care to admit, usually with one hand holding the lighter and the other trying to make sense of a sentence I wasn't ready to finish. Most of these pieces were born in the middle of the night. You know the kind—when your head's spinning too fast to sleep, and the only thing left to do is write it out before it eats you alive. That's where this came from. Survival instinct dressed up in syntax.

The goal to turn this into something tangible by my 30th birthday didn't come until later; when I realized I needed to prove, mostly to myself, that I could finish something. That I could take the mess and give it form. That all the almosts and what-ifs and burned-out nights could be more than memory. That they could be made real. Permanent. That I could hand it to someone and say, "Here. This is what I've been doing with the heartbreak. This is the proof I lived through it."

There's no clean genre for this. It's poems, essays, lists, voice memos in disguise. Some of it is sharp, some tender. Some of it feels like pressing on a bruise. Some of it reads like the punchline to a joke I'm still trying to understand. But every piece in here is honest. Even the ones I want to take back. Especially those.

I called it Ashtray Etiquette because that's what it's felt like...learning how to live gracefully among the wreckage. How to sit in the ruin and still light something beautiful. How to carry grief like a clutch purse, like it matches your outfit. How to look someone in the eye after they've seen you cry on your bathroom floor and still say, "I'm good. Want a drink?"

This isn't a self-help book. It won't tell you how to heal or who to block or when to start over. It's just what I had to say before I turned 30. It's my proof of life. My little time capsule of hope, delusion, obsession, silence, rage, beauty, and the occasional stroke of accidental clarity.

So read it out of order. Read it when you feel like a mess or when you feel like a god. Read it when you can't tell the difference. I wrote this to stay alive. I wrote it so it could live longer than the moments that created it. I wrote it because I needed somewhere to put all the versions of myself I didn't want to throw away.

Welcome to *Ashtray Etiquette*.

Take what you need.

Flick the rest into the tray.

And if nothing else,

light one for me.

Section Index

Section 1:
Mental Notes From The Edge

Female Hysteria

I came out fists first.
Screaming like the world slapped me
and I slapped it back.

Nobody tells you
a girl can be born
already sparking.
Like a flare already lit.
Gunpowder on her breath.

Hysteria.
As in the Greek word “hystera”
or *uterus*.
To keep it clinical,
containable.
A diagnosis you can sip with your tea.

But I am not a subdued science.
I am a tsunami.

I am a bar fight in a ballet dress.
Lipstick smeared on a courtroom floor.
Mud under manicured fingernails.

They say I spiral.
I say I orbit.
I say I cyclone.
I say I cracked the world open
and found the devil himself
pacing around down there.
Even he couldn't handle it.

Unfortunately for most,
women like us don't burn out.
We black out entire cities.
We unscrew stars
with our bare hands.
We are the reason some men
sleep with the lights on.

Call it hysteria

if your mind can't handle

words like power

or hunger

or *no.*

But remember,

witches were just women

who saw the flame,

lifted their chins, and said

Do your worst.

Strategies For A Parallel Universe

Eat the manual.
Don't read it.
It's written in the dialect of regret
and poorly translated optimism.

Names are assigned at random.
Yours might be Margot Saint Rogue.
Answer to it.
Authority here respects compliance
over self-awareness.

If the floor feels soft,
keep walking.
You're not sinking,
you're being assessed
for density.

Emotions cost extra.
You'll be invoiced quarterly.

Eye contact is currency.
So is spit.
So is silence,
but only when weaponized correctly.

People walk backward
on Thursdays.
Try not to comment.
It's considered rude
to acknowledge the choreography.

If offered a map,
fold it into a paper crane
and set it on fire.
Destination is a myth
perpetuated by those who sell luggage.

Love is archived.
You can request access,
but there's a waitlist.
And you'll have to sign a waiver

about side effects:
insomnia,
misremembered endings,
repetition.

Don't panic
if your limbs glitch.
Most realities don't sync
until the fifth or sixth visit.

Dreams must be submitted
for content moderation.
Violent fantasies are allowed.
Hopeful ones
require a sponsor.

Don't bother packing.
Whatever you need,
you'll forget.
Whatever you bring,
you'll lose.

Whatever you miss,

you didn't deserve.

If you make it out,

don't write a book.

No one believes escape stories anymore.

Minor Acts Of War

We hurt ourselves in ways
too polite to count as damage.

Not with blood.
Not with drama.
But with the daily betrayal
of staying
in places we've already outgrown.

In letting texts go unanswered
just to punish someone
who wasn't even waiting.

In loving people
who treat us like vending machines,
easy to access,
forgettable once empty.

I stayed.

That was the first wound.

I swallowed silence

like it was discipline.

Told myself I was loyal

when I was just afraid.

The mirror kept showing me

a version of myself

that winced too easily

and smiled too often.

I laughed at jokes

I didn't understand.

Touched people

who never learned my middle name.

I carried the deadweight of hope

like it was sacred.

Built futures

on things he only said when drunk.

Healing isn't a poem.

It's a habit.

A brutal one.

No climax.

Just choices.

Small ones.

Over and over.

I've done the sabotage.

The long-distance denial.

The "it's fine" when it wasn't.

The apology I didn't owe.

The shrinking.

I forgave too soon.

Left too late.

And called it love.

But I'm done being collateral damage

in my own story.

Let the minor wars end.

Let me come back whole.

Not because I escaped,

but because I stopped setting the traps.

A Bastard Called Insomnia

2am is always asking questions that shouldn't be answered at 2am.
Like,

why can't you sleep?

is it insomnia?

or mania

or that pill that you took too late in the day

or that text you didn't receive

or that place you want to move to

or that movie that terrified you last week

or that your pillow feels foreign

or that there's nostalgia for something not quite specific

or that you're terrified of your own brain

or that you don't know what love is

or that you do and may never experience it again

or that you're wasting time thinking about it

or that you should probably just call him

or that your mom is looking older

or that you don't travel enough

or that you need to take your car to the shop

or that you have no savings account

or that you have no roots and no plans to plant any

or that you want to run away from yourself

or that you forgot to eat dinner again

or that you'd love to be held

or that you want to call your sister

or

that it's 2am?

And maybe it's just

insomnia.

Things We Do To Avoid Feeling

– Blame astrology or the moon

– Scroll until our thumbs go numb and our eyes blur

– Sleep with people we can't stand

– Bleed into art we'll never show anyone

– Pretend we're "working on ourselves"

– Wander into bad habits like they're old lovers

– Swallow the hard stuff with no water

– Build our identities around damage

– Chain smoke outside dive bars

– Disassociate in scalding showers

– Buy new shit we absolutely don't need

– Call our mom for light gossip and validation

– Treat our bodies like rental cars

– Turn apologies into bad jokes

– Book therapy sessions to cancel

– Cling to mania like a parachute

– Falsely try to turn indifference into strength

The House Bipolar Built

It’s not that I break.
It’s that I rebuild with strange blueprints.
That one morning I wake up drywall,
and by nightfall I’m stained glass.

I am the house bipolar built.
Shaky foundation,
but god, the view.

Mania is the architect
with a cocaine habit and a god complex.
He paints my ceilings gold
and tells me I can fly.
He throws glitter on my wounds
and calls it healing.
He turns lightbulbs into suns,
and suddenly every room is worth dancing in.

I love him.

He loves me.
Until he doesn't.

Then depression moves in
with a U-Haul of regrets
and a playlist called
"just lay down for a minute."

She turns off the lights,
boards up the windows,
sits on my chest like rent is due.

Together,
they redecorate my brain
every six days.
New wallpaper.
Same haunted hallways.

I have left fingerprints
on people who only wanted postcards.
I have spoken in tongues

and apologized in therapy.
I have kissed with matches in my mouth
and called it foreplay.

Sometimes I am not a house.
I am a hurricane.
Other times I am the porch light,
flickering gently,
just trying to say:
someone's still home.

And some days,
on the good days,
I am a structure worth staying in.
A quiet hallway.
A room with a breeze.
A welcome mat that doesn't lie.

This isn't a tragedy.
It's an open floor plan
with unpredictable lighting.

So no,
I don't need fixing.
I need visitors who understand
that sometimes
I redecorate mid-sentence.

And that doesn't mean
I'm falling apart.

It means I'm still here,
rebuilding.

Daily.
Loudly.
In color.

Checklist For When The Mind Leaves Without You

Find the body.

Hopefully yours.

If it's upright and wearing pants,

you're already ahead of schedule.

Conduct a wellness check.

Are you blinking?

Are you rinsing dishes that were already clean?

Are you signing emails

"Thank you!," like you mean it?

Confirm absence of mind.

If you're thinking about

2009,

or that man who said "I'm not ready,"

or death,

but in a casual, Tuesday kind of way,

she's gone.

Eat something.

Not because it'll help.

Just to prove you still have the hands for it.

Attempt grounding.

Name five things you can see.

Forget the names.

Swear tacitly.

Move on.

Identify landmines:

scents that remind you of people

you shouldn't still be mourning.

Voicemails from your dead grandmother.

The word "eventually."

Consider therapy.

Then remember your last therapist

had a smoker's cough and said "mmm" too often.

Decide silence is cheaper.

Check the clock.
It's 3:17.
Again.
As always.

Stare into space
like it's the next episode of Grey's Anatomy.
Forget what you were doing.
Forget what you were supposed to feel.

If possible,
reenter the body.
If not,
hover nearby.
Supervise your own detachment
like an underpaid manager
on her second divorce.

Repeat as needed.
(And it will be needed.)

File it under:

“Functional, Technically.”

Or “Tuesday.”

Same difference.

The Only Sin I Won't Repeat

There was a time I thought failure was external. Something you could measure in negative account balances and unanswered messages, and that heavy, sour quiet that clings to a room like the stench of spilled whiskey and regret.

But that wasn't failure. That was life. Blurry and hungover and occasionally cruel. I know better now. Real failure is almost silent. When you're splitting yourself into digestible pieces and contemplating putting yourself down like a sick dog. It happens when you start walking out on your own soul and calling it maturity.

Self abandonment. The only real failure in this life. And the only sin I won't commit twice.

If I go down now, I go down swinging, with my gut intact and my eyes clear. If I fail, I'll fail filthy, bloody knuckled, truth in my mouth, full weight of myself intact. This body, this voice, this fury, this tenderness...I'm never handing it over ever again. You want easy? Buy a houseplant.

And that version of me, the one who kept abandoning herself just to be wanted?

She's dead.

I buried her with no eulogy.

No flowers.

No fucking apology.

Advice I'd Give If Anyone Bothered To Ask

Don't trust anyone who says
they've never been jealous.
That just means no one's ever
cut them open properly.

If your gut says no,
it's already packed a suitcase.
Let it leave.
You'll catch up to it eventually.

If you wake up
and don't recognize your reflection,
leave her be.
She might finally
know what she's doing.

If it's running,
it probably wants to be gone.
Let it go.

Time doesn't heal.
It just makes the memory
harder to prove.

Beauty fades.
Wit sours.
But a woman who knows how to vanish
is dangerous forever.

Cry if you must.
But cry with intention.
Nothing sadder than a woman
who weeps out of habit.

The lucky devil isn't the one
who gets the girl.
It's the girl who learns
she doesn't need to be gotten.

And when the world
starts screaming at you,

try whispering back.

Sometimes,

it shuts up

just long enough

to listen.

Sleeping On Wet Hair

Sleeping on wet hair
always felt like inviting spirits in.
Like cracking the window
and daring the past to crawl in
with cold hands and unfinished sentences.

It's the kind of recklessness
that looks innocent.
A damp pillow,
a chill you can't place,
a dream you wake from
with someone else's name in your mouth.

I've loved men
who showed up like hauntings:
unannounced,
unsettling,
familiar in the way
a shadow knows your shape.

Best friends who thought I was healed
because I stopped bleeding on the daybed.
Lovers who mistook my quiet for safety
and left when the house settled wrong.

I have curled up in blueprints
of futures that never got built,
slept in beds
that whispered other women's names.

I have been the afterimage
of a woman worth staying for,
the kind you remember
when your next life feels too quiet.

But still,
I dry.
Grief doesn't cling forever.
Even fog knows when to lift.

Tangled, yes.

But intact.

Let them say I'm too much.
That I carry storms into sleep
and make the bed smell like memory.

I'd rather be haunted
than hollow.
I'd rather carry the ghosts
than become one.

So no,
I won't wait to dry off.
I won't ask for safety.
I sleep soaked
in what I survived
and wake up
unapologetically alive.

Your Depression May Vary

Walking the dog feels like a hostage negotiation
between willpower and muscle.
He waits by the door.
I stare at my shoes across the room.
Neither of us wins.

The shower's been running for an hour.
My hair stays dry.
Washing it feels like a four part tragedy
with no witnesses to move along the plot.

I go to work.
Mascara, coffee, a whisper of Adderall.
Five milligrams of permission
to function, or at least show up.
Sometimes that's enough.

I let calls go to voicemail.
Mom. Best friend. Sister.

I love them,

but their voices ask too much.

If I sit still too long,

I'll forget how to stand.

If you give me the whole weekend,

I'll turn into furniture,

go fully catatonic.

But I'm fine.

I've got the script down.

I'll call my psychiatrist.

I'll take the extra meds.

I'll send the "sorry, just saw this" text.

I'm fine.

I'm *always* fine.

My hippocampus is just glitching.

I can't remember what joy felt like,

only that I once had it

and now I stare at things

that should move me

but don't.

Not even a twitch.

Everything feels like I'm underwater

looking at the world

through a window smeared with grease.

People talk.

I nod.

I have no idea what anyone just said.

But I still get up.

Still move through the motions.

Answer what I can.

Refill the little orange bottles.

Hold the toothbrush like my life depends on it.

Cry when it comes.

Scroll until the ache fades.

I haven't quit yet.

This isn't drama.

This isn't poetry.

This is *just a rough patch.*

This is *just a downswing.*

This is *just something everyone deals with sometimes.*

This is just depression.

User experiences may vary.

Just Enough Ruin To Function

I don't want to be healed all the way. People forget that.

Total recovery is boring. You lose your edge, your reason to eavesdrop in coffee shops, your excuse to cry during commercials.

I want just enough ruin to write well. To still laugh at the wrong moment. To still run my fingers over the jagged marks and remember what gave them to me.

I want to function, sure. But with a limp. With a bruise shaped like a city I should've never left.

Give me progress, but make it uneven. Let my growth be clumsy. Let my joy be vicious, bitten around the edges.

I've spent too long trying to be whole when I was never meant to be symmetrical.

I am a mosaic.

And some of my best colors came from the cracks.

Apologies In Advance

Sorry I've been a bit feral lately.
I forgot I'm allowed to ache
without putting it in a polite pale dress.
I forgot that disappointment
doesn't need a permission slip.

I know, I've been hard to reach.
But the world is blazing in hazy focus,
and I'm still expected to open Outlook
and remember my Hulu password.
The apocalypse is oddly bureaucratic.

Apologies for being all teeth and no tongue lately.
Totally slipped my mind
that I don't have to clap for crumbs
or thank men with a parade celebration
for clearing the bare minimum.

Sorry I've seemed distant behind the eyes.

It's been a season of watching power dynamics
implode on us.
Accountability is extinct,
and my patience died right there with it.

I probably seem like I'm boiling over.
Like I've swallowed a storm
and let it ferment.
But tell me,
what's the right amount of rage
for a woman expected to be palatable lately?

It's not you.
It's probably just me.
It's probably always just me.

So sorry again for...everything.
Eventually, I'll crawl back
into something resembling composure.
But it won't be today,
probably not tomorrow either.

Just a heads up.

Apologies in advance.

Section 2:
Injuries Caused By Connection

My Mind's Mannequin

It's a goddamn circus in here,
and he's the ringmaster.
A mannequin in my skull.
Wearing that corduroy jacket I love and
an expression I can't forget
even though I've tried
with wine, strangers, and three months of good behavior.

He doesn't speak.
He just paces.
Sometimes taps on the glass
like he's got a point to make.
But it's always just a bit of lint
masquerading as meaning.

He clogs the air vents with static,
rewinds the highlight reels on loop,
throws a tantrum whenever I flirt
with a fresh perspective.

I gave him a lease,
once,
a humble space in the attic of affection.
Now he's installed purple velvet ropes and
a disco ball
and started charging admission
to my own attention span.

I bought candles to replace him.
Therapy. Journals.
Even once dated a man with warm eyes
and no ghosts.

I think he likes
the echo chamber he's built
out of my doughy parts.
Wears my loneliness
like a tailored suit.
Mumbles familiar phrases
while I dream of silence.

And he still paces.

But the glass is one-way now.

Let him watch.

The Bar

The bar isn't low.

It's subterranean.

I've tripped over higher expectations

in gas station bathrooms.

It's rusted, crooked,

last seen supporting a man

bragging about therapy

like it was a life-altering crisis

he survived

and not just

four sessions and a co-pay.

They want praise

for basic decency.

For responding.

For not lying this time.

For saying "I'm working on myself"

as if that means

they've put anything
on the damn workbench.

They say they're different.
They mean different from the men
they used to be,
but not different enough to matter.

They want the poem.
Of course they do.
They want their reflection
tenderly rendered
in iambic pentameter.

But god forbid
you ask them
to show up
without a disclaimer
or a caveat
or a reason they "need more time".

I've done the crawling thing.
On floors and toward men
who thought "effort"
meant not hitting on your best friend.

I'm too old
to hand out gold stars
for bare minimum behavior
disguised as growth.

Bring me substance.
Bring me contradiction,
but at least be brave enough
to name it.

And if you can't manage
depth
or decency,

stay the hell
out of my poems.

The Classifieds

Single woman.

Still breathing, mostly.

Must tolerate:

- Mood swings sharp enough to cut you

- Nights that don't end until something breaks

- A history she doesn't bother hiding

Side effects:

- Walks out mid-sentence

- Sleeps with one foot out the door

- Misses people she shouldn't have met

Details:

- Trusts no one who smiles too easy

- Spends money like it grows back

- Collects regrets like old stamps

Offering:

- Half-smoked cigarettes
- Old wounds she calls souvenirs
- A laugh that doesn’t mean she's happy

Warning:

She’ll leave before you even notice she was there.

Or worse: she’ll stay just long enough to ruin you too.

Apply drunk.

Stay sober.

Good luck.

Terms of Engagement

She didn't torch his world.
Too obvious.
Too merciful.

She left no smoke,
just absence.
Which, frankly, hurt more.

He woke up one day
to find her gone,
and nothing missing
except the pieces of him
she took as proof of engagement.

She didn't cry.
She didn't spiral.
She plotted.

Reassembled her spine

with steel rods.
Carved out the rot
he left in her.

Then she bloomed:
louder,
meaner,
unapologetically wrong
in all the ways he hated.

He watched from the sidelines
as she became everything
he tried to edit out.

She started showing up
in rooms he didn't control.
Took up space
like a riot in all black.

Every time he tried to speak on her,
she imagined people laughed.

"She dated you?"

Like it was a punchline.

He became trivia,

a cautionary blip

in her origin story.

She didn't need revenge.

She was the revenge.

And that was more than enough.

Things To Romanticize

– The loneliness of hotel rooms

– Books that have been relentlessly dog eared

– Blackened knuckles and bitten lips

– The last sip of wine in a glass

– The first inhale after crying

– Lipstick stains on coffee mugs

– Making eye contact with strangers

– A single light left on in an empty house

– The last song played at a party

– Bare feet on wet pavement

– The moment before lips meet

– A flickering neon sign on a silent street

– The lingering scent of someone's perfume

– A slow dying bonfire

– The hum of a vinyl record before the music starts

– Catching the twinkle of a star with your naked eyes

Twenty Two Night Stand

He asked for a ride home.

What he meant was,

"Let me disappoint you again,

but in a way that feels familiar."

He never said it.

Of course he didn't.

Men like that think implication

counts as intimacy.

I unlocked the door anyway.

I always did.

Habit is a hell of a drug.

We drove in silence,

him playing DJ with his future excuses,

me counting the red flags

like mile markers.

We were "friends."

Which meant

I let him use my body

like a therapist's couch,

and he repaid me

with compliments

so vague

they could've been meant for the dog.

No declarations.

No demands.

Just a choreography of almosts

performed under dim lighting.

Afterwards,

he'd smile like he invented restraint.

I'd ask,

How long are we going to keep doing this?

He'd smirk.

That smug, slippery smirk

men wear when they know

you'll let them stay
even after they've already left.

He said I was easy to be around.
Which meant
I never cried when I should've.
Never asked
if he saw anyone else
or thought about my laugh
when it wasn't echoing off these walls.

It wasn't a relationship.
It wasn't not one either.
It was a holding pattern,
a layover,
a cushioned place to land
until he remembered
he didn't want to be caught.

He never remembered my birthday.
But he remembered how my perfume smelled

and thought that was enough.

He always left early,
before the sheets cooled,
before I could say
stay
without it sounding like
a plea.

I dropped him off
like junk mail.
He kissed me and said goodbye.
Then just shut the door
like punctuation.
A period, not a question mark.

I lit a cigarette,
watched the smoke
fail to mean anything profound,
and drove home
with a chest full of expired hope

and no one left to give it to.

Not love.

Not even lust.

Just a man who didn't know

how to leave gently,

and a woman who forgot

how to lock her damn door.

The Other Kind Of Jealousy

It wasn't about her boyfriend.

Or her job.

Or the way she always found parking.

It was about how light she moved.

How she didn't shudder at being seen.

How she cried in public and didn't apologize.

She said things I only thought of later.

Wore yellow on days I hid in gray.

It wasn't envy in the traditional sense.

I didn't want her life.

I wanted her soul.

I wanted to feel as free in mine as she looked in hers.

We were friends.

Of course we were.

Best friends, truly.

I loved her.

But I also hated how she could just be.

No backstory.

No disclaimer.

No need to explain why her joy didn't feel like theft.

I never said anything.

Until I said everything except that.

That's how women are trained.

You tuck the jealousy under your tongue

and swallow it with a smile.

And then you compliment her.

Men I Don't Say The Names Of Anymore

They're boxes in a back closet,

labeled badly,

sealed with tape that won't stick.

I don't visit.

One was a mama's boy

who called it loyalty.

Another called me beautiful

but never asked me how I slept.

One prayed after fucking me

like I was a problem

only God could fix.

They all wanted

a girl who forgave quickly,

who didn't notice

while their promises

dried out and died prematurely.

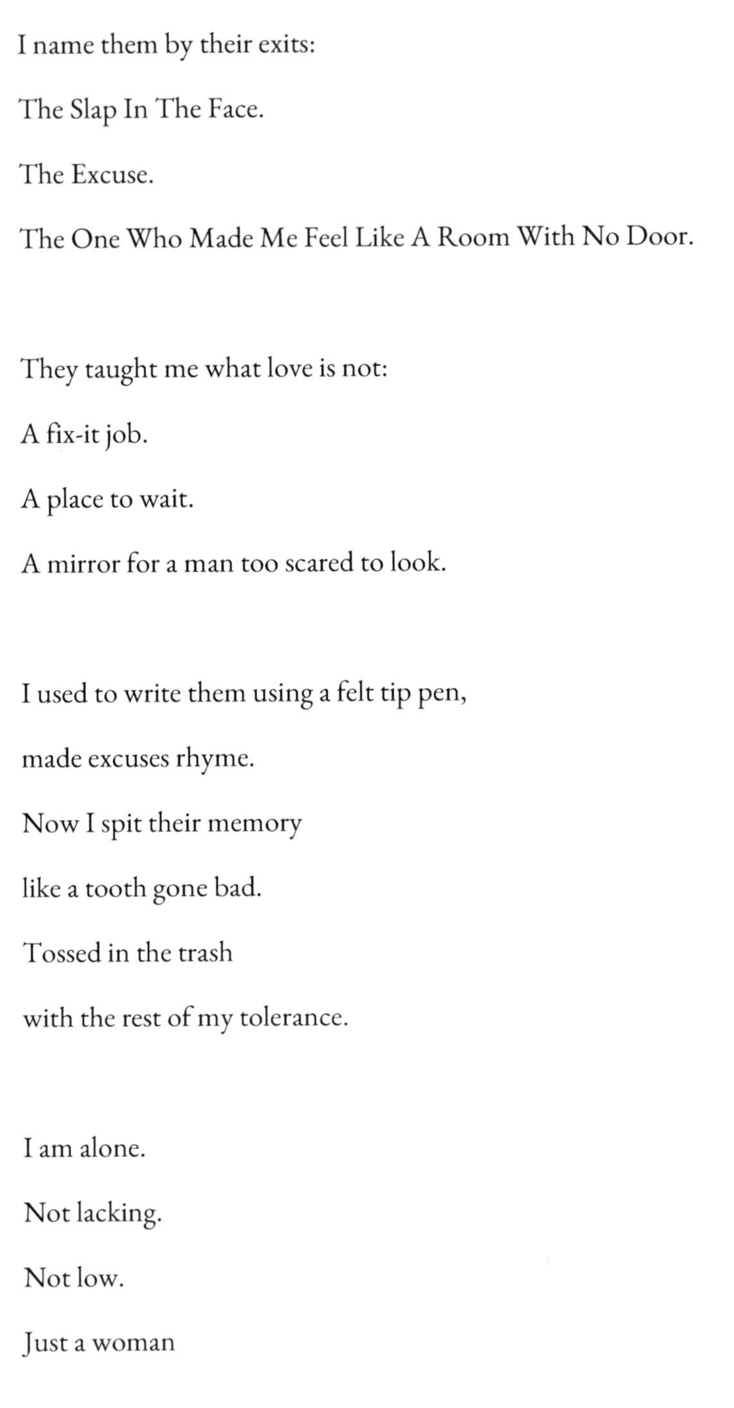

I name them by their exits:

The Slap In The Face.

The Excuse.

The One Who Made Me Feel Like A Room With No Door.

They taught me what love is not:

A fix-it job.

A place to wait.

A mirror for a man too scared to look.

I used to write them using a felt tip pen,

made excuses rhyme.

Now I spit their memory

like a tooth gone bad.

Tossed in the trash

with the rest of my tolerance.

I am alone.

Not lacking.

Not low.

Just a woman

with both feet planted,

a vocabulary like a trucker's,

and no interest

in being anybody's maybe.

Guilty Pleasures

– Pressing bruises just to feel the ache

– Windows down with the heat blasting

– The smell of freshly poured pavement

– Dingy pubs

– Boutique hotel rooms with big bathtubs

– Secret eye contact

– Cheap gas station sunglasses

– Yacht Rock playlists

– Wearing perfume to bed

– Coffee & champagne for breakfast

– Leaving the candles lit for too long

– Winking at strangers for no reason

– Book endings that annihilate your heart

– Opposites who attract

– People who talk in their sleep

– Playing devil's advocate

– Talking about the weather

– Falsely believing we have control over anything at all

Mama's Boy

The first time,

he made drinks in New York

like he was mixing ambition with ice.

Said he wasn't like the others.

And I believed him.

Because lies are easier to swallow

when they wear cologne

and lean in close.

He talked like he'd escaped something.

Like he'd run from the marble prison

his family built on old money and thin blood.

Said he wanted to earn it.

Said he loved me.

Years passed.

We lived five minutes apart in L.A.

Didn't know it.

The universe must've been drunk.

When he found me again,

I mistook the apology

for growth.

We played house.

We played healed.

We played each other.

Then came the voice of his mother

in his mouth.

The verdict from people

who'd never met me.

"I just can't go against them."

Like he was drafted.

Like he had no say

in his own fucking life.

He left. Again.

The sequel no one asked for.

Trust fund puppet

with a great head of hair.

Tried to gaslight me
into thinking it was my fault.
As if cowardice
wore a cape.

He was never mine.
He was theirs.
A son,
a legacy,
a disappointment
in designer clothes.

And me?
I'm no longer waiting
for a man
to choose me over his mother.

I don't date auditions.
I don't rewatch flops.
I don't mourn people
who confuse loyalty

with obedience.

He's still playing himself.
Still convincing strangers
he's deep.
Still soft-spoken
with a paper heart.

But I'm not angry anymore.
Just deeply
and endlessly
unimpressed.

Sleepovers Don’t Fit Me

I never liked sleeping at someone else’s place.

Your sheets smell like detergent I don’t use.

Your air tastes different.

The water pressure is unpredictable.

And still, I let myself be convinced.

That closeness is worth the discomfort.

That warmth is worth the disorientation.

But I always end up awake at 3am,

on the edge of a too-firm mattress,

staring at the ceiling like it’s going to tell me a secret.

I tiptoe to the bathroom.

Open drawers I shouldn’t.

Read the labels on your prescriptions.

You don’t stir.

Of course you don't.

Men like you always sleep through the parts that matter.

In the morning, you'll ask if I slept okay.
And I'll lie.
Because it's easier than explaining
how foreign I feel in a bed
that doesn't know my shape.

I'll leave before noon.
You'll say we should do it again sometime.
And I'll nod,
already knowing
that I won't last in these conditions.
Especially not in borrowed spaces
where nothing fits,
and I'm expected to rest.

What I Meant To Say Was

I meant to say...

You were the scab I kept picking at

because it felt good to be exposed.

You were the heat before the storm hit

that vibrates around you like a warning.

You moved like a man with no address.

Half human, half performance art.

I kept forgetting to give your clothes back

because it meant one of us had to return.

Twenty nine hit me with brass knuckles.

No fireworks, no more regrets,

just a pair of high waisted jeans

that finally fit just right and the creeping knowledge

that you still weren't coming to fix anything.

Not my mess.

Not my hunger.

Not the piece of me you kept stealing and giving back.

I wanted to say:

you talk like someone who's never been slapped for it.

You called me complicated

like that was a reason to leave

instead of a map to follow.

I didn't want you to love me.

I wanted you to wreck me.

I wanted to come apart in your hands

like a cassette tape unspooling,

blaring something sad and low-budget

from the dashboard of your leased personality.

What I meant to say was:

I would've held you gently if you let me.

What I meant to say was:

Why can't you keep me?

What I meant to say was:

Fuck you.

I love you.

Section 3:
How To Be A Person (Instructions Not Included)

What Satisfaction Never Touched

There are days I wonder if I was built wrong. Not in a tragic, Shakespearean way, just slightly off, like someone misread the blueprint and poured the foundation crooked. I'm not unhappy, exactly. Just perpetually underfed, like I keep showing up to life's banquet dressed for the wrong meal. Everyone else seems to have cracked the code. Matching dishware, partners who stay, weekend plans that sing with purpose. Meanwhile, I move through my own life like a trespasser, flipping on the lights and hoping it feels like home.

My friends talk about their baby's nap schedules, their husbands' quirks, the equity they're building. They host potlucks and bring things that require actual recipes. I bring wine and a vague sense of universal dread. It's not envy. I don't want their lives. I just want mine to stop feeling like something I'm auditioning for. I want to stop hovering six inches above everything, watching it unfold with the aching sense that I was supposed to be somewhere else by now.

I've tried to land. In people, in cities, in jobs my parents were excited to brag to their friends about. I've slept beside warm bodies that couldn't melt the ice inside me. Lit expensive candles in apartments that never quite fit me. I've clung to fleeting highs and called them meaning, only to watch them dissolve like sugar in rainwater. It's not that I think I'm better. I just think I was built for something I haven't met yet...or maybe something that doesn't exist.

Maybe some of us weren't built to be content. We were wired to feel too much, too often, too hard. Not broken, just struck like a match.

And the hunger? I pray it's not a weakness. Maybe it's the engine. The thing that keeps us always searching, reaching, becoming.

The Milestones That Get No Applause

– Eating three meals in a day

– Washing your hair before it tells you to

– Remembering to check the mail

– Finally doing the laundry instead of just buying more socks

– Getting gas before the light gets dramatic

– Answering your friend's text without spiraling about the delay

– Only smoking four instead of five

– Using just one exclamation point in an email

– Paying rent on time

– Actually taking your car to the shop

– Sleeping through the night without chemical intervention

– Going to the gym after a long day

– Remembering your parent's anniversary

– Calling the doctor instead of googling your demise

– Flossing

– Not checking your ex's social media accounts

– Saying "I'm not free" without explaining why

– Not needing a crisis to clean your room

– Not requesting permission to exist today

The Customer Is Always Wrong

Welcome to Purgatory & Co., where we exchange broken souls, misplaced identity, and any lingering resentment from your last lifetime.

How can I pretend to help you today?

No, we don't carry closure. Try aisle five, next to the expired affirmations and unfinished apologies. If you hit regret, you've gone too far.

You say it "looked different online"?

Of course it did.

Everything does.

That's the algorithm.

No, we don't offer refunds for time wasted.

We recommend journal prompts.

Or denial.

Oh, you'd like to exchange your anxiety for inner peace?

Let me check the inventory.

Nope, we're out.

Although we do have yoga with a side of dissociation

and a therapist who asks "where do you feel that in your body?"

This coupon expired in 2018.

Right around the time you stopped trusting yourself.

We can't honor that.

You broke your boundaries and now you'd like to return the consequences?

Relatable.

Still no.

We're happy to take your self-awareness,

but only if you're ready to replace it with delusion.

That's the only even trade we offer.

We do have a new self-improvement bundle:

– Fake forgiveness

– Repressed anger in travel size

– And a bottle of lavender-scented suppression.

No, it doesn't work.

Do you have a rewards card?

Ah.

Still waiting to be rewarded for existing.

You and everyone else.

Listen:

We can't fix you.

We can't unmake the choices.

We can't relabel what you loved as "a learning experience."

But we can offer you store credit for your next spiral.

Just show your receipt.

It's probably in your Notes app.

Right between

your grocery list

and

"things I should've said."

Friday, The Reckoning

Friday is the cigarette you swore you'd quit.
But there she is, leaning smug in the doorway,
wearing the red dress of forgiveness.

She doesn't ask what you've done all week,
just pours you a glass,
kisses your shoulder,
and lets the silence thrum like bass
in the chest of a dying party.

She arrives like a crooked prayer,
answered by mistake,
or maybe on purpose
by a god with a drinking problem.

She's not Sunday, all sermon and shame.
She slips in through the crack
between exhaustion and delusion,
whispers, *you made it*, as if survival were the same as living.

But the truth is,

you didn't survive the week.

You postponed the reckoning.

And yet somehow,

it felt holy.

The Drug Of Daily Horoscopes

I don’t necessarily believe in it.
But I show up anyway.
Daily.
Desperate.
Like a junkie scouring the alleys
for my next existential fix.

I check three sites.
Cross-reference like a conspiracy theorist
on no sleep.
If two say *doom* and one says *desire*,
I take the liar.
Hope’s never needed to be honest,
just loud enough to drown out reason.

Today, the stars say
you’re on the brink of transformation.
Which could mean
I’m finally going to quit him.

Or maybe just that I'll order a salad for lunch
and pretend it's a lifestyle change.

It's all code,
vague enough to hit where it hurts.
Avoid confrontation.
Too late.
I already texted back.

Some days it tells me to rest,
as if sleep is something
I still get invited to.
As if my brain doesn't scream
like a car alarm all night
when I think about forever.

But still,
I read.
Because the universe has better bedside manners
than my therapist.
And astrology is the only bastard

that tells me my minor mania is endearing.

I don't need it to be right,
I just need it to *say something*.

I need it to say
you'll figure it out,
you'll be wanted,
you'll be worth the fucking mess.

And when it doesn't?
I scroll again.
Switch apps.
Spin the wheel one more time.

Call it delusion.
Call it comfort.
Call it a daily ritual
for the chronically lost and confused.

But don't call it dumb

until you've stared down your own damn fate

and begged it

to *just say something back.*

Things I Do In Case Of A Happy Ending

– Rip the tags off

– Buy the champagne

– Leave the door unlocked

– Bring the extra cigarettes

– Leave my makeup on

– Order the dessert

– Wear the heels

– Bet the whole bag

– Laugh too loud

– Take the everything shower

– Light the good incense

– Take the photo

– Lose the map

– Say it first

– Trash the plan

– Spill the secret

– Show up late, stay too long

– Take the blame

I Sent My Feelings Through TSA

They flagged my carry-on.

Said something looked unstable.

Probably the loneliness...I packed it without thinking.

Wedged between two unfinished thoughts

and a sweatshirt I don't wear unless I miss someone.

They asked me to unzip it.

I warned them.

Said it's mostly unresolved shit and emotional contraband.

But they were already putting on gloves.

Out spilled the usual:

a few sharp thoughts I keep pretending don't draw blood,

a recurring memory I won't admit still wrecks me,

the kind of longing that gets you banned from birthday parties.

They held up a bottle of self-sabotage.

Too many ounces.

I said, "Keep it."

They looked relieved.

They examined a tangle of texts I never sent.
Saw the one that said "No, really, I'm good" three different ways.
One of them was almost convincing.

A younger agent found the guilt.
Tried to fold it back neatly.
Didn't know it unravels if you touch it wrong.

Then came the grief
safe inside a ziplock, stuffed inside a cosmetic bag,
still pulsing like it doesn't know it's not alive anymore.
The agent recoiled.
Said it should've been declared.
I said it's always been carry-on only.

Finally, they pulled out the love I don't talk about.
Held it up like evidence.
It looked heavier than it used to.
Cracked down the middle but still ticking.

I said nothing.

They sealed the bag.

Zipped it quickly and quietly.

Cleared their throat.

Said,

"You're good to go.

Just... maybe check it next time."

I nodded.

Took my bag, my shame,

my boarding pass with the coffee stain.

And walked toward the gate like I hadn't just been unpacked by strangers.

The conveyor belt kept moving.

It always does.

In Favor Of Dropping The Act

I've worn charm like a choke collar. Slipped it on every morning like armor disguised as lipstick. Smiled with all my teeth and none of my intent. That's the first mask: likability. It fits best when you're breaking.

Then there's competence. Starched, polished, vocabulary elaborate. The mask they clap for. The one you wear when you're two panic attacks deep but still answering emails like you're thrilled to be alive. That one's heavy. Straps dig in. But God, it photographs well.

There's a mask for family dinner. Where you laugh at the right moments and pretend you haven't thought about disappearing. There's the party mask, smeared with gloss and good intentions, made to last until someone asks, "How have you been?" and you say, "Busy," because "barely breathing" is apparently bad small talk.

Sometimes I wonder if I have a real face under it all, or just layers of crowd-pleasing costumes. Am I the version that wins at happy hour small talk, or the one that chain-smokes through 3 a.m. silence? Am I the girl who keeps her cool in insanity, or the one who locks herself in the bathroom and breathes into a towel?

I really don't take the masks off. I rotate them. Like records in my collection no one's danced to in years. They still spin, hoping someone remembers the sound.

But lately, I'm tired. Tired of smiling without reason. Tired of being digestible. Tired of adjusting the bass levels of my truth just to keep the room comfortable. I want to peel it all off. Leave the masks in a pile by the door. Let the world meet the version of me with no stage directions.

And if they turn away?

Let them. I'm done tapdancing in someone else's skin.

Gut Instincts And Other Liars

I have trusted my intuition like a drunk trusts their own reflection.
With unwavering, idiotic confidence.
I have mistaken stomach flips for soulmates,
thinking: *surely no organ would betray me like this.*
Followed my gut into the arms of people
who only loved me in lowercase.

I have boarded flights I could not afford
to cities where no one knew my name,
certain that anonymity would taste like freedom.
It mostly tasted like overpriced martinis
and waking up unsure which side of the bed was mine.

I have quit things prematurely,
convinced that restlessness was a spiritual calling.
Turns out, it was just an undiagnosed panic disorder
and a tendency to romanticize chaos.

And yet, for all her heedlessness,

my intuition has led me to gentle landings.
Made me linger a second longer before crossing the street.
Made me say yes to the last-minute decision
where I met someone who would hold my name gently.

So I will keep following her.
Even when it leads me into locked doors
and temporary lovers.
Even when it feels like being blindfolded
and spun in circles.

Because sometimes, when I least expect it,
she leads me home.

Sundays, My Lover

Sundays slip in like a familiar ex,
the one who never asked too much of me.
They arrive in yellow morning light,
smelling faintly of last night's dreams
and lemon detergent.
I let them in without brushing my hair.

The New York Times sprawls on the coffee table,
all self-important and crinkled.
I read it slowly, even the boring parts.
Obituaries of strangers I pretend to miss.
Book reviews I'll forget to buy.
It feels poetic, somehow.

Coffee is hot and unreasonably strong,
like it's been up all night overthinking.
The dog snores beside me,
his belly warm under my heel.
My soulmate who doesn't know my first name.

I light incense called something like Ancient Forest
that smells nothing like the trees.
The gray clouds climb the walls slowly,
like they have nowhere else to be.

I refuse to make plans.
I leave texts on read.
I exist solely in the radius of my living room.
I play new vinyl on an old record player.
I romanticize the laziness,
call it restoration.
Call it a religious experience.
Call it mine.

The Cruel, Quiet Sport Of Waiting

Waiting is the most exhausting thing I've ever done without moving. It's not heroic, like endurance; it's not graceful, like surrender. It's a purgatory of maybe. A liminal hallway where the light flickers, and you're never sure if you're about to walk through a door or vaporize entirely.

People talk about patience like it's a virtue, but I think it's a slow form of madness, an itch under the skin of time. You sit in the stillness pretending it's peace, but really you're bargaining with the void.

Waiting feels like holding a door open for someone who might never come in. Eventually your arm goes numb, your smile cracks, and you start wondering if you imagined the knock.

But still, we wait. Because what else is there? To stop waiting feels like betrayal. To move on feels like treason. So we sit. We fidget. We try to make art out of absence.

But here's the hard truth I keep in my pocket like a stone: waiting doesn't always mean something is coming. Sometimes, the wait is the thing. Sometimes, the silence is the answer. And sometimes, the only way out is through...through the boredom, through the ache, through the unbearable intimacy of wanting something that does not want you back.

Yet.

Seasonal Work

Some mornings, I make eggs like a woman
who flosses every night and never feeds the wrong inner wolf.
I take my shoes off at the door,
play Billy Joel through a speaker that's lived its own life,
and balance the bills like a tightrope walker
with just enough faith in the wire.

Other days,
I'm spitting out metaphors on an empty stomach,
chasing shots of caffeine with low-grade dread,
wearing yesterday's transgressions around my waist.
I water the plants just enough
to keep them in the mood to suffer.

There's no rhyme to it,
no lesson tucked under my toes.
Just the tide, in and out.
Some weeks I write ballads in my sleep,
all but grazing God's stubble with my fingertips.

Other times my sentences limp out of me,
seeming to barely survive the fatal event of being formed.

Routine is a rumor I keep trying to believe.
Havoc, a roommate who always drinks my almond milk
and leaves notes on the mirror like
you were born to be feral,
stop pretending you like serenity.

Somewhere between
the sixth therapy session
and the seventeenth theoretical undoing,
I learned that thriving isn't a place,
it's a flash in the pan.
A sexy joke told in good lighting.
A moment of good reception in the valley.
Just a warm season in the ebb and flow.

Things The Angel On Your Shoulder Might Be Busy Doing

- Taking her smoke break

- Untangling the threads of fate

- Catching all the words you nearly said in a basket

- Sewing up the cracks in your heart

- Slipping love notes into your thoughts

- Alphabetizing your past lovers

- Sipping whiskey with your silence

- Humming your grandfather's favorite song

- Tucking hope under your pillow

- Writing small kindnesses on your lips

- Sitting in mediation with the devil

- Brushing dust off your old dreams

- Hiding strength in your bones

- Weaving light into your darkness

But Mostly I've Been At Home

I've been taking inventory of my vices,
dusty ash and sticky spills.
The kitchen clock is stuck at 3:17,
and I haven't fixed it because
it feels honest.

The days don't really pass,
they drag their knees on the floor,
wearing yesterday's eyeliner
and last week's intention.

The dog doesn't mind.
He still thinks I'm the best part of this apartment,
even when I'm chain-smoking
in nothing but my oldest T-shirt,
thinking about the men
who slipped out like fog in the night.

I drink now,

but not like I used to.

It's lighter.

A slow bourbon,

a glass of red that gets forgotten on the windowsill.

I toast to the quiet.

I toast to the war I'm not fighting anymore.

Mostly, I've been at home.

Writing like someone's listening,

though I know they aren't,

not yet.

My days have become

a series of sentences

with no punctuation,

but an alarming sense of rhythm.

Outside, the world clicks and spins

like it knows where it's going.

Inside, I am trying to matter

in the slowest way possible.

Without applause,

without climax.

I keep waiting
for the switch to flip.
For the lights to come on.
For the world to decide
I'm finally worthy
of something massive.

But for now,
I write.
I drink.
I pet the dog.
I ash into vintage glass trays.

So yes,
mostly,
I've been at home.
Wilting inward,
but still leaning toward the sun.

Let's Play With Fate

I've lived in cities where I cracked molars on midnight choices and stitched new myths into my mouth like gold fillings. New York, where I waitressed next to a strip club and kissed a man with a stitched-up eyebrow who was not my boyfriend. L.A., where I tried the same love for the second time like it was a food allergy test. Didn't take. My love's always had side effects.

People like to ask me what I'm "looking for." As if I misplaced it in the trunk of my car next to my twenties. I'm not looking for anything gentle. I've had gentle, and it wilted in the heat. I want something brutal in its honesty. I want someone who sees me at 4 a.m. leaking gin & tonics with a credit score that's bleeding out, and still says, *Stay*.

I don't want clean narratives. I don't want safety. I want the spark that singes the eyebrows off. I want the kind of jolt that rattles your fillings and changes your handwriting. I want to peel the world open and crawl inside its worst parts just to see if there's still a rhythm pulsing beneath the rust.

Fate and I, we've circled each other like stray dogs. She's bitten me more than once, but I always came back with a bigger bone to pick. She doesn't play fair, but neither do I.

Still, I say *let's play*. Let's bet everything on a bad idea just because it screams louder than the good ones. Let's take the job that doesn't make sense, chase a voice we only heard through a wall, say yes to the invitation still hot from a stranger's hands. Let's write the poem that gets us in trouble. Let's kiss the wrong person and make it count.

Section 4:
The Things That Tether Us

Voicemail Of The Universe

You've reached the voicemail of the Universe. I'm currently spinning at 67,000 miles per hour and still somehow behind on everything. If this is about your purpose, your person, or your parking spot, please know your message is very important to me and will be ignored in the order it was received. For karma, press 1. For chaos, press nothing and wait.

If this is a plea for clarity, I recommend flipping a coin or sleeping on it until the answer shapeshifts. If you're calling to ask why, please hang up and scream into a pillow like everyone else. If you're seeking closure, try a candle or a haircut. If you're calling about that feeling you can't name but can't shake...yes, I put it there. You weren't supposed to notice it yet.

Leave your yearning after the beep. Or don't. I already know what it says. I am the missed connection, the glitch in your gut, the static between thoughts. Speak, if it soothes you. But don't expect a reply. I've never been one for linear conversation.

Estimated response time is typically one heartbreak, two revelations and one lunar eclipse.

Thank you for your patience and have a pleasant awakening.

Guaranteed Expiration Date

Death's not subtle.

She's been leaving you clues.

The hair in the drain.

The way your knees sound when you stand.

The avocado that went bad in one day flat.

You keep saying

"next week,"

like you've got a private extension.

Don't forget you're going to die.

It's not a threat.

It's a fact.

Like your hangovers getting meaner,

or you turning into your mother.

So wear the shirt with the weird pattern.

Quit the job you tell your friends is killing you slowly.

Make the awkward phone call.

Make the fucking art.

Say I love you even if it's three drinks in.

Time doesn't wait.

Neither does death.

And neither should you.

The Women Who Save You

Not all at once.
Not with confetti or rescue boats.
But with dry shampoo,
a well-timed meme,
and the ability to remember
your mom's maiden name
and the date your life fell apart.

Not loud like lovers,
not planned like promotions,
just there one day,
quietly saving your life.

They see you in fluorescent lighting,
bare-faced, unraveling,
grieving men who didn't know
what they had in their hands.
And they don't ask you to be graceful.
They just pass you the takeout,

crack open the wine,

and let you fall apart

on their favorite sweater.

These are not background characters.

They are front row,

arms raised,

screaming for you at every finish line

you didn't even think mattered.

They remember your big days

and your tragic ones,

your ex's dog's name (Finn)

and the scent of your corner store shampoo.

Lovers will write you poems

and forget your favorite cocktail order.

But these women?

They'll carry your secrets in their glove compartments,

answer your calls on their worst days,

and text you back

while crying in a Whole Foods parking lot.

They're not your other half.

They're the whole damn net

beneath the high-wire act

of becoming yourself.

And if you are ever loved

fully,

without requirement or performance,

it is by them.

It *is* them.

Modern Day Addicts

It's not addiction
if it's functional.

Caffeine before consciousness.
Adderall to fine-tune the caffeine.
A glass of wine to take the edge off,
a second to take the edge off the first.

We're not numbing,
we're optimizing.
We track our sleep cycles
while ignoring the fact
we haven't really slept in years.

We double-tap strangers
for serotonin,
answer emails at midnight,
text like lifelines,
sleep beside the glow

of dying phones.

We don't smoke,

except on weekends.

Except when we're anxious.

Except when it's raining.

Except always.

Champagne like it's hydration.

Vape like it's a quick snack.

Melatonin, magnesium,

CBD, THC...

alphabet soup to knock us out

without asking why we can't rest.

We call it "aesthetic."

We call it "routine."

We say we're biohacking,

not unraveling.

Our therapists are on retainer.

Our livers, on overtime.

Our parents still don't know

we microdose before brunch.

It's not dependency,

it's *wellness.*

It's not avoidance,

it's *hustle.*

It's not panic,

it's just a high-functioning disaster

with a well-designed calendar invite.

No one stages an intervention

for the girl in a matching workout set

with a reusable water bottle

and a 10am meeting.

Nobody's worried

as long as we pay rent on time

and keep our breakdowns quiet.

Buzzed, not broken.

Just a little chemically blessed.

We're not addicts.

We're just coping

in acceptable packaging.

God's Performance Review

If there is a God (and I'm not saying there is, but hypothetically, for entertainment purposes) then it's time we talked about performance. Not worship, not faith, not mythos. Performance. Job output. Results. Deliverables. Because if God were an employee, they'd be overdue for a check-in. Not a prayer, not a hymn, a quarterly review. And honestly? Mixed feedback.

Let's start with the highlights. Creation was an absolute banger. Galaxies? Gorgeous. Platypuses? Delightfully chaotic. Human consciousness? Bold move. And let's give credit where it's due: sunsets continue to slap, and orgasms, on a good day, are arguably better than most spiritual experiences. God clearly has an eye for drama: the ocean is loud, volcanoes are sexy, and the whole birth-death-love-ruin cycle is undeniably cinematic. Points for aesthetic. Strong branding overall.

But the gaps in performance are hard to ignore. The customer service model is, frankly, unresponsive. Prayers are ghosted. Miracles are rolled out inconsistently, like beta features in a broken app. Natural disasters seem poorly timed. The entire free will initiative was clearly launched without proper ethical vetting, and the system still hasn't been debugged. Most damning of all: evil continues to be outsourced to humanity, and no follow-up has been scheduled.

And yet, for all the mess, something about the job remains oddly compelling. Maybe it's the mystery. Maybe it's the refusal to explain. Maybe God is less of a manager and more of an artist—volatile, stubborn, elusive—and we're just the poor souls trying to interpret the abstract installation piece that is existence. If that's the case, fine. But the least they could do is send a memo. Or a sign. Or an apology. Until then, we'll keep showing up, filing complaints, and calling it belief. Performance: inconsistent. But unforgettable.

Places We Find Ourselves Again

- In the crack between the bathroom door and the floor, knees on the tile

- In the silence of a movie theater, while the credits roll

- In the backseat of a stranger's car, hands pressed against the window

- In the back of a dive bar, with a drink you didn't pay for

- In a hotel room with peeling wallpaper and a bed that's seen better days

- In a laundromat, watching clothes spin in endless circles

- In your childhood bed alone, with your parents in the next room over

- On a balcony in a foreign city, watching the sun rise over rooftops

- In a tattoo parlor that smells like antiseptic and rebellion

- In a fast-food drive-thru, your stomach filled with guilt

- At the bottom of a pool, eyes wide open

- In the corner of the eldest part of the cemetery

- In the eyes of your sister, reliving your past mistakes

- Sitting at your desk at work, writing this list for you and everyone else you love

Field Notes

I didn't mean to intrude.
Didn't mean to overhear
the way she asked
softly, like borrowing air,
for more time together.
And how he blinked like she'd demanded
a Fabergé egg
wrapped in legal custody.

It's a habit of mine,
this listening.
In coffee shops.
On barstools.
Through the polite paper walls of public restrooms
where people cry,
laugh,
and occasionally pray into their elbows.

Call it a tether.

A thread.

A lazy spirituality.

God never talks to me directly,

but he does whisper through

other people's bad timing.

I've heard things.

A man with hair plugs

and a woman barely of age

booking a villa in Tuscany.

The wife unaware.

The assistant complicit.

The lies laminated.

An artsy boy,

twenty-something and full of audacity,

explaining to his father

that once the Amex

covers "a few more months,"

his painting of a melting clown or

a bleeding rose or something else cliche
will definitely go viral
and finance the revolution.

And once,
a little girl with cookie on her cheek
asked her nanny,
“Why does Mommy need
so much wine?”
The nanny didn’t answer.
Just tied her shoe tighter
like that might help.

I don’t insert myself.
I just collect.
I archive the real and the raw,
the unguarded and stupid,
like pressed flowers
from someone else’s season.

I never tell.

Except here,
in poems.

So no,
I didn't mean to intrude.
But you should've seen
how tragically she broke
right in front of her chai latte.

How could I not watch?

Things I've Done Instead (Part 1)

Called my mom about nothing.

Tried to do a headstand.

Took four Advil for half a headache.

Bought cherries just to tie the stems with my tongue.

Failed.

Accidentally swallowed a cherry pit.

Tried to learn French on YouTube.

Gave up after 11 minutes.

Scrolled through dating apps.

Deleted them all.

Swore off men until I'm 40.

Trimmed my dog's bangs.

Searched all my exes on Instagram.

Deleted Instagram.

Reinstalled Instagram.

Called my mom again.

Read four pages of a book.

Googled "News that isn't about Trump".

Took a bubble bath.

Smoked a cigarette out my kitchen window.

Listened to experimental jazz on Spotify.

Searched Pinterest for Bukowski quotes.

Posted one.

Deleted it.

Went for a walk.

Decided it's too hot to be alive.

Wondered about the process of cremation.

Rewatched the same Seinfeld episodes.

Set the smoke alarm off trying to cook dinner for one.

Apologized to my neighbors for waking up their baby.

Took another bubble bath.

Thought about a martini.

Thought about London.

Thought about my grandma.

Did a skin care routine.

Decided it's not working.

Over-plucked my eyebrows.

Took some melatonin.

Drank the tea with the bear on the box.

Listened to classical music.

Asked the universe why I can't ever sleep.

Wondered about "god".

Kissed my dog's tiny forehead.

Told him I loved him and meant it.

Turned on a white noise app.

Turned it off immediately.

Made a list of all the things I've done instead.

Called it poetry.

The Geometry Of Intimate Moments

The half-second too long of eye contact,
just enough to make you wonder
if they'd destroy you beautifully.

The first bite of someone else's food,
because it always tastes better when it's stolen.

The quiet *tsk* of a lighter sparking,
right before they lean in to share the flame.

The small, sacred pause
before the song starts and the crowd roars.

The split-moment glance at someone
when they're not looking,
subtle and unguarded,
like you've caught them being human.

The way their voice sounds when they're half-asleep,

all gravel and satin.

The slow thud of a book falling shut on your chest
as you doze off with the stars.

The shared blinks
when someone else is talking,
the quiet thrill of your own private language.

The worn-in ritual
of splitting the last of the wine in a bottle.

The ache of knowing
some moments are meant
only for the losing.
But we keep on chasing.

An Ode To Guilty Pleasures

Who decided that pleasure needed an apology? That the things that make us feel alive must also make us feel small? I have never once heard a man whisper, "I know it's foolish, but I love power." I have never once seen someone ask forgiveness for their ambition. And yet, we bow our heads over our joys, tuck them into the pockets of our shame, let them decay in the dark.

But pleasure, true pleasure, does not care for permission. It does not ask to be reasonable. It exists in the marrow, in the hunger that makes us human, in the quiet defiance of choosing salt in a world that worships sweetness.

So, I am done feeling guilty for the things that make me feel. I will sink my fangs into the flesh, drown in the forbidden cravings, lose myself in the fantasies that let me believe, if only for a moment, that life can be oh so satisfyingly taboo. I will love my indulgent behaviors, my melancholic daydreams, my masochistic nostalgia. I will love them without restraint, without explanation, without shame.

Because I do not exist to be measured.

I exist to crave, to consume, to smolder.

Lessons From The Desert

The desert teaches us
that there is wholeness in solitude.
A kind of quiet defiance
in never watering herself down
just to make someone else feel quenched.

Pale, but relentless.
Like cashmere with a spine.
Silent, but stretching endlessly.
A presence you don't forget
just because she says nothing.

She welcomes the ones who see her beauty
without needing her to bloom on demand.
And to the rest?
She offers nothing but the grace of distance.

Unmoved. Unmasked.
She is the most admirable enigma.

Not for her mystery,

but for her refusal

to be anything other than exactly what she is.

Controlling Feral Cats (And Other Illusions)

There is a moment (usually during the 2 AM insomnia where overthinking, existential emergency and too much Adderall converge) when you realize you are gripping life too tightly. White-knuckled. Breath held. Scratching at outcomes as if they are obligated to you.

There is a kind of violence in clinging too hard to what we think should happen, breaking our own hearts over narratives that never stood a chance. We live in the fear that if we stop holding our breath, we will somehow freefall into ruin.

The tragic, hilarious truth? We were never in control to begin with.

You see, life is more of a feral cat than a well-trained dog—it does not care for our planning, and it certainly won't sit on command. It darts in and out, unpredictable, sometimes purring, sometimes clawing, and all we can do is offer it the freedom it demands.

And oh the dripping seduction in letting go. The days you stop playing god and start playing human. Choosing to believe that what is meant for you will not need to be wrestled into submission. It will arrive, quiet and certain, and it will stay because it was always yours.

So, here's to pure release. And surrendering to the unraveling...untamed, intricate, and breathtakingly imperfect. Yet always falling into place.

Things I've Done Instead (Part 2)

Googled "famous people with bipolar disorder".

Booked a dentist appointment.

Canceled it an hour later.

Started making a playlist called "Not For Sober Ears".

Filled it with songs I've sent to men I used to love.

Tried to call my brother just to say hi.

Went for a drive to the gas station.

Bought Skittles and a Vanilla Coke.

Didn't smile back at the cashier.

Wondered if astrology is real.

Thought about moving back to LA.

Remembered how much I hated it there.

Got the hiccups, but only for a minute.

Secretly hoped for a meteor to hit earth.

Searched "property for sale in the Mojave Desert".

Checked my credit score.

Wasn't surprised.

Sent three memes in a row to my best friend.

Ignored her last eight text messages.

Checked flights to Australia.

Added silk bed sheets, $55 skin cream, and dog treats to my Amazon cart.

Checked my Capital One banking app.

Took everything out of the cart except the dog treats.

Closed my laptop for the night.

Put on a pot of decaf.

Started watching Casablanca at midnight.

Thought about that one time with that one guy at that one bar.

Wondered if he'd remember me.

Knew he would and then stopped caring.

Fell asleep with my socks on and dreamt of nothing.

The Decline Of Wanting More

There was a time I wanted everything.

The top of the corporate ladder.

The dream apartment.

The kind of lover who says your name like it's expensive.

I read self-help like scripture.

Set alarms to "manifest."

Said affirmations with a cracked voice and hopeful gums.

I believed in vision boards and hustle culture.

Said yes before I meant it.

Networked like it was for my health.

Worked like someone was grading it.

Now?

I want coffee that's strong.

Mornings with no dread.

Friends who text back.

I don't want to be a mogul.
I want to be okay.
Whatever that means in a world
that profits off your inability to sit still.

The "ambition" leaked out slowly.
Not all at once.

It evaporated
on Sundays when I skipped the gym to blissfully sip wine,
on Thursdays when I chose to write alone vs attend the mixer,
on quiet nights when no one was watching
and I didn't perform productivity.

It wasn't a breakdown.
It was a choosing.

And people don't understand it.
They ask if I'm "still chasing the dream,"
if I've "lost momentum,"
if I'm "settling down."

They think peace is a backup plan.
That stepping off the carousel means you're weak,
or worse, unambitious.

They mistake stillness for failure
because they've never known rest
that wasn't laced with guilt.

I used to call it burnout.
Now I call it perspective.
A personal, silent revolution.

I'm not lazy.
I just stopped needing to be impressive
to anyone but me.

Sometimes, consistent contentment
is the loudest kind of success.

And if they can't hear it,
who am I to mess with the volume?

Theories On The Universe

I have theories about the universe, as everyone does. Some people say it's expanding, stretching itself thinner with every passing second, as though it's a pair of leggings that've been worn one too many times. Eventually, it'll split at the seams and leave us all with nothing but a cosmic wardrobe malfunction. Others, the more romantic ones, believe in a multiverse. A collection of parallel universes where everything we didn't choose, every tiny "what if," is playing out in some alternate dimension where you're probably rich and happy, or maybe just a sentient blob of stardust wondering where it all went wrong.

Then, there's the favorite theory of the truly nihilistic: the universe doesn't care about you. Not one bit. It's cold, indifferent, a random set of particles colliding into each other for no reason at all. Heat death, they call it. The universe eventually freezing into a quiet, endless night, where nothing happens, because there's no one left to care. It's the universe's way of saying, "Yeah, it was fun for a while, but I've got better things to do than hold your hand while you completely lose your grip."

My favorite theory...what if the universe actually does care? Not in some benevolent, mystical way, but in the most absurd, overwhelming way possible? Maybe it's like that one friend who loves you too much, so much that it makes you uncomfortable, makes you wonder how long you can keep pretending it's not suffocating. Maybe the universe gives you everything it has, over and over, until you're not sure if you're grateful or just sick of it.

In the end, none of it makes sense. The universe isn't out here trying to give us answers. It's too busy being big, and old, and unfathomable. And we're just here, trying to figure out how to make ourselves matter, even though we know, deep down, it's probably all one big cosmic joke. But maybe the joke is this: we keep looking for meaning, when all along, the meaning has been that we're still here. Stumbling, wondering, existing.

And in that, perhaps, is the only theory worth believing.

Things I'd Say At My Own Funeral

- Don't say "she's in a better place." You have no idea where I am. Neither do I. Let's not lie at my funeral.

- You don't have to pretend I was always kind. I was frequently tired and sometimes rude. But I tried. Most days. That should be enough.

- To my dog (if he outlived me): You were always the best man. Sorry I never let you eat the pizza crusts.

- I didn't accomplish everything I wanted to. But I loved harder than I planned to, and that's something.

- Look under my bed. That's where I hid the good notebooks and some very questionable Polaroids.

- Please tell my therapist I was trying.

- If someone reads one of my poems, make sure it's not the one I wrote just to impress someone who didn't love me back.

- I forgive you. Even if you think I shouldn't.

- Don't clean up too quickly. Let the mess sit for a while. Let it ache. That's part of the love.

- I'm not watching over you. But I hope something strange and warm reminds you of me when you least expect it.

- If anyone says "she wouldn't want us to be sad," know this: yes, I would. Cry. Wail. Bring the drama. Then go eat cake and kiss someone hot. That's the point.

- Keep living like it's temporary. Because it is. That's not the curse, it's the miracle.

The Architect Of Accidents

There is no god here.
Just gravity,
and the way I keep falling into things
that feel too perfect to be coincidence
and too fucked up to be divine.

I don't pray.
I leave voicemail-length thoughts
to an unnamed force,
a kind of cosmic drunk dial
to whatever's been pulling the strings
with such exquisite recklessness.

I don't want answers.
I want proof that the chaos is curated,
that the mess of my life
was designed by something
with a dark sense of humor
and a fetish for inevitability.

I don’t believe in destiny,
but I do believe in patterns.
In the way one bad night
can ripple through five years,
turning strangers into mistakes,
and mistakes into the holy grail.

I believe the universe is a street magician.
Quick hands, dirty nails,
pulling threads I didn’t know I was tied to,
laughing while I stumble
into exactly what I needed
without knowing I wanted it.

There’s no worship in me,
just a grudging respect
for how everything lands
exactly wrong enough to be right.

If there’s a god,
they’re not watching.

They're in the back,
playing poker with my choices,
stacking fate like chips,
and letting me lose just enough
to keep the game interesting.

No, I don't believe in God.
But I believe in the architect of accidents,
the great cosmic shrug
that sends me reeling
into the next disaster
I was always meant to survive.

Section 5:
It's Called Transcendence, Baby

Rules For Transcending

– Kill the timeline they sold you.

– Grieve like an animal.

– Do not turn work into salvation.

– Romanticize your own destruction.

– Expect betrayal.

– Use your affection like a loaded gun.

– Let the dead things die.

– Learn the art of disappearing.

– Use rage as fuel, not foundation.

– Sleep with whoever the hell you want.

– Do not, under any circumstance, chase closure.

– Let bitterness ferment, then pour it out as poetry.

– Remember that money will never feel like enough.

– Aging and loving should both be done violently.

Before I Became Who I Am

I was everyone's favorite mirror.
Reflecting, not feeling.
Saying "I'm good" before checking the inventory.
I didn't know what I liked.
I knew what got applause.

I was smaller, yes,
in the way a file gets compressed,
all potential crammed into
a format no one could open.

I answered every knock,
even when it was just the wind testing the hinges.
Thought every shadow was a messenger,
every tender spot a curriculum.

I was duct tape over a leaky valve.
Not a fix, just delay.
Pressure building.

People called it passion
because they couldn't hear the hiss.

I believed pain made things honest.
Believed if it hurt,
it meant it mattered.

I was sad in the kind of way
that made people uncomfortable at events.
Not tragic. Not palatable.
Just weird and seeping
and unsure how to sit right in a chair.

I didn't know what intuition felt like.
Only what adrenaline felt like.
Ran every red light
because at least the blur felt like movement.

But,

I was never weak.

Just underused.

Like a fire escape that never felt feet fleeing.

I was me before.

But diluted. Muffled.

Offered up in pieces like samples at a market.

Now I'm full price.

I require certification to handle.

Proof of experience in fast paced environments.

Before I became who I am,

I was still me.

But raw.

Untranslated.

I still am.

Only now I observe my own patterns,

and withdraw before contamination occurs.

The Vanishing Act

Somewhere along the way, I misplaced her. The girl I used to be. She didn't vanish in a blaze of glory or a final, cinematic goodbye. She slipped quietly between the couch cushions of time, like a receipt from a life I no longer live. I didn't notice until I went to reach for her, and found only echoes.

It's a strange thing, not remembering who you were before. Before the heartbreak, before the job, before the slow rot of routine and resignation. Before you learned to pretend you didn't care so much. Before you stopped dancing in the kitchen just because the kettle whistled.

Sometimes I catch glimpses. A laugh I didn't mean. A craving I forgot I used to have. But mostly, she's a myth I tell myself when the present feels too unrecognizable.

It's not all tragic. There's something honest in the forgetting. Maybe we aren't meant to stay loyal to the old versions of ourselves. Maybe the girl I was had to be left behind so I could survive the next chapter. Maybe remembering is less important than becoming.

Still, on quiet nights, I wonder if she misses me too. If she ever thinks of the future and sees me. Older, quieter, stranger. And hopes I've kept something of hers...a pastel kindness, or maybe a flashy spark.

I hope I have. I hope she'd recognize me. Maybe not by my face, but by the way I still reach for the light, even when I don't know where it's coming from.

Things You Don't Have To Tolerate

- Low quality wine

- Apologies without action

- Advice from people who've never had to start over

- Cheap bed sheets

- Men who say "I've just been so busy lately"

- Friends who require constant cultivation

- Spending on name brand perfumes

- The bare minimum

- Therapists who say "let's unpack that" without intention of helping

- Diet culture

- Wedding invites from people you haven't spoken to in over a year

- People who ask when you're going to settle down

- Dressing room mirrors

- The phrase "high maintenance"

- Oversharing with people who didn't earn it

- The idea that healing should be graceful

- False urgency

- Shrinking yourself into versions others find palatable

Proof Nothing Is Wasted

The flight you missed by seven minutes.
The one you cursed and lost your peace over.
It kept you in the city long enough
to walk by a man playing Leonard Cohen on a rusted guitar.
And long enough to realize
you are still someone who stops for music.

The plants you keep forgetting to water.
They're still there.
Proof that things can forgive you
even when they shouldn't.

The two years you gave to the wrong person.
Everyone says they were a waste.
But they don't know
how you learned to love through gritted enamel.
How you mastered the art of leaving quietly.
How you stopped apologizing for taking up space.

The song you only listen to when you're a little bit drunk.
The one that ruins you in the best way.
You've played it 74 times
and it still hasn't fixed anything.
But you keep trying.
And that counts for something.

The poems you wrote for people
who didn't deserve them.
They still belong to you.
They are still yours.
And you were always worth writing about.

Nothing is wasted.
Not even this.
Not even now.
Not even you.

Ashtray Etiquette

There’s an elegance to igniting things,
isn't there?
The way a match flares up,
full of promise,
then dies,
leaving nothing but ash.
A trail of abandoned desires,
just like us.

I’m learning how to crush my thoughts
under the heel of the present.
It’s a delicate thing,
this ashtray etiquette,
like flicking the last bit of yourself
into a forgotten corner
where it doesn’t matter.

I’ve perfected the art of half-smiles,
of stubbing out a thought before it becomes

too real.

It's not about the fire,

it's about the pause,

the knowing quiet between the exhale

and the next cigarette.

And maybe that's all we get.

The quiet flicker of an ember

before the world moves on

and leaves us,

still warm,

waiting for the wind to find us

and blow us on

to our next destiny.

Drink Your Water

My dad tells me to drink more water. Says it like it's the cure for whatever you've got. Fatigue, heartbreak, cancer...whatever it is, water will fix it. He says it gently, with the same tone he used when I was twelve and wouldn't stop picking at mosquito bites until they scarred. Like he's hoping if he repeats it enough, I'll stop bleeding at the edges.

There's something strangely intimate about the way he says it. Like he's trying to hold the last thread between us steady. He doesn't ask if I'm happy. Doesn't ask if I'm still seeing that person I told him about in passing months ago. Doesn't bring up the time I told him I feel like I'm always ten minutes behind my own life. He just tells me to drink water.

There's a specific kind of decay that sets in when you hit your thirties and realize most people don't love you the way you thought they would. They stop calling. Not because they're cruel, but because they're tired. Everyone's just trying to exist. So you learn to stop expecting. You learn to shake a little quieter.

But my dad, he keeps calling. Keeps asking about my car, the weather, my sleep. And always, Are you drinking water?

It's funny, the older I get, the more I understand the things he doesn't say. He doesn't traffic in metaphors like me. But he knows something about keeping your bones from giving up before your mind does. And maybe that's the point. Maybe hydration is a stand-in for all the ways we stay tethered to the planet when we'd rather float off it.

Sometimes I listen. Sometimes I drink the water. I stand at the kitchen sink in the middle of the night and gulp it down like I'm trying to fill every hole I've carved out of myself. Like I'm trying to stay.

And maybe I am. Maybe I'm trying in the only way I know how. Not with affirmations or crystals or a morning routine, but with tap water at 3 a.m. with the lights off and my feet cold against the tile.

But it's a start.

Save One For Me

I hope you unhinge your front door
like it's a bad habit you've finally outgrown.
Toss it into the street. Let the wind in. Let the world see.
Let them hear you scream until your voice goes hoarse
and their polished little lives start to rattle.

I hope you learn to love your loneliness.
Not like a burden, but like a decadent nightly ritual:
a cigarette curling into the bathroom ceiling,
your knees slick with bubble bath and clarity,
feeling just as satisfied as the first time
you mistook fantasy for a future.

And when you cry, because you will,
I hope you pause,
consider bottling the tears,
just to salt the rim of your next martini.
Drink yourself in like a sacrament.
Like you're the only truth left worth swallowing.

And with no door to muffle your brilliance,

I hope they scatter,

the ones who only ever came for the quiet version of you.

Let them run.

Because the ones who stay,

the ones who don't scatter at your storm,

they'll know how to sit at your table,

match you drink for drink, tear for tear.

And if it's just you,

yourself and the aftershock,

I hope you save one glass.

Leave it on the counter.

I'll be there soon.

Lost And Found

I've lost parts of myself in places that don't do returns.

A laugh in a Nashville bar bathroom.

The ability to trust someone who talks too much with their hands.

Half a backbone in someone else's broken bed frame.

We all do it.

We shed. We crash.

Not because we're careless,

but because we believe

someone will find our missing pieces

and return them.

The problem is, most people take souvenirs.

They hold onto the best bits

and pretend they've earned them.

And by the time you ask for them back,

they've already sewn them into the sleeves of their skin.

Still,

there are days you spot a version of yourself
hitchhiking in someone else's story.
Not waving, not dying to be rescued,
just thumbing her way through the wreckage,
grinning like she knows the plot twist.

And maybe you don't want it back.
Maybe you don't want the laugh,
the trust,
the fucking backbone.

Maybe you want the open tab.
The stretch of highway.
The freedom to never be returned to sender.

So you stop leaving breadcrumbs.
You stop checking lost and founds
for versions of yourself that left
on purpose.

And in that empty space,

no resolution,

no redemption arc,

you start building a new self

with nothing but broken pieces and borrowed tools.

And she doesn't ask for the missing parts.

She lights another cigarette,

names herself something unpronounceable,

and walks off the edge of the map.

The War After The War

Why did no one disclose

that staying soft would feel like a suicide mission?

Anyone can build walls.

Anyone can weld anger into armor

and call it moving on.

It's easy to dissolve inside your own defenses,

call it *healing* when it's actually *hiding*.

Hardness demands nothing.

It just survives.

But softness,

softness is a violent, reckless thing.

Softness means stepping into the wreckage

barefoot,

knowing damn well there's glass on the floorboards.

It means loving again

with the cut still wide open.

It means setting down the knives

before you're sure the threat is gone.

Softness is not for the innocent.

It is not for the naive.

It is for the ones who know exactly

what it will cost them

and still choose to risk it anyway.

But eventually,

you'll get tired of the armor.

It doesn't breathe well.

It chafes in places you forgot were still uncalloused.

So one day,

you'll try softness on again.

You'll laugh too loud.

You'll flirt back.

You'll let someone see your kitchen

with the dishes piled high in the sink.

And just like that,
you're exposed.

A raw thing.
A risk.
An open invitation.

Giving yourself back to the world,
walking back into battle
chest first and
blissfully unarmed.
Ready for the next war.

Sometimes I Miss L.A., Always I Miss New York

L.A. was a faint lie I told myself.

A filtered dreamscape.

Palm trees swaying like they knew something

I never would.

Everyone there was selling

a version of themselves

and I was stupid enough to buy one,

shrink-wrapped and sun-drenched,

with just enough serotonin

to keep me sedated.

I left fingerprints on glass I never shattered.

I left voice notes in tones I don't remember.

I lost my laugh in a canyon,

trying to echo someone else's purpose.

God, I was beautiful there,

but I wasn't mine.

New York was different.

She didn’t hold my hand.

She handed me a MetroCard and said,

"Run or rot."

So I ran.

I bled for her.

I sobbed on sidewalks and still made it to work by 9 AM.

There were rats and roaches and

mornings so cold I questioned every life choice.

But at least it was real.

At least I was.

I found friends who weren’t afraid to see me cry,

found strangers who knew my name

before I told it.

Found fire escapes to exhale my thoughts on,

and rooftops that felt like churches.

I fell in love on a Friday.

Got my heart broken on a Thursday afternoon.

Heard the city weep with me that night

in the quiet hum of Brooklyn.

Sometimes I miss L.A.

the way you miss a fever.

Brief, delusional,

and strangely warm.

But always...always I miss New York.

She never pretended.

She never tried to save me.

She just handed me a pen

and dared me to write something

with no fear of retribution.

The Beauty Of Solitude

No one tells you
that being alone
is a kind of aristocracy.
You get the whole goddamn kingdom.
Dripping faucet, unpaid electric,
the silence thick as a silk noose.

No one double-dips in your sorrow.
You drink it neat,
from a chipped teacup
that used to belong to your grandmother
or someone you thought you'd marry.

Solitude is a motel bible
with the pages torn out,
a sermon written in eyeliner
on the bathroom mirror:
"You are the final draft."

It's cooking pasta for one
in just your bra and panties,
steam making your pores bead with sweat
like some feral elegy to hunger.

No one asks
where you've been.
And no one lies
about missing you.

Being alone
isn't lonely.
It's a penthouse suite
at the end of the world.

You become fluent
in the language of buffering signals,
grow fond of the smell
of something slightly burning,
and start to trust
that no witness

means no interference.

And that

is the benefit of being alone.

You become

the punchline,

the poet,

the king and the queen all at once.

Things It's Okay To Outgrow

– The apology in your voice

– Plans made by your younger self

– Your hometown

– The urge to shrink for comfort

– The fantasy of being understood

– The craving for closure

– That old pair of jeans that gaslight you

– People you once would have bled for

– The illusion of permanence

– Political views that don't fit you anymore

– Old bars you lost yourself in

– Nostalgia that harms more than it soothes

– Lovers that feel like bad habits

– The romance of self destruction

– The routine of mistaking pain in the chest for passion

– The fear of outgrowing things

Plot Writers

There's a moment, just before everything goes sideways,
when the air goes still,
and we always lean in.
We never step back.
We've never once mistaken caution for virtue.

We've done things we won't explain
to people who wouldn't understand anyway.
We've left good places for worse ones
because the light hit differently
or the silence got too honest.
We've made decisions out of instinct,
out of ache,
out of the kind of hunger your mother wouldn't understand.

People think we're impulsive.
They say it like it's a flaw.
But they forget:
disaster has always made the better story.

We don't live for safety.
We live for the scene.
For the rooftop confession,
the too-long eye contact,
the secret you'll have to take to the grave.

And yes,
we've broken hearts.
Our own, mostly.
We've driven through cities we should have flown over.
Lost nights to things that felt right at 4 AM.
We've said "this is it"
a dozen times
and meant every single word.

You could call it recklessness.
We call it living with intent.
The intent to feel everything.
The intent to write the kind of life
that kills us in the most romantic way.

We know it'll end badly.

That's not the point.

The point is, we wrote it.

Every mess. Every miracle. Every scene.

We're not the heroes. We're the plot writers.

And God help the editor.

Made in the USA
Columbia, SC
06 August 2025

c1aed985-fdd3-4dbf-9f76-df5f122d1f64R01